Erotica short stories for women erotica stories & erotica book for women & men to increase lust

Erotica for men and women erotica romance & erotica fantasies Bedtime stories for couples or singles

© / Copyright: 2018

Cortney Manocchia

1st edition

ISBN: 9781717709929

Self-published

Print: Amazon Media EU S.à.r.l., 5 Rue Plaetis, L-2338, Luxembourg

The work including its parts is protected by copyright. Any use is prohibited without the consent of the publisher and the author. This applies in particular to electronic or other duplication, translation, distribution and public disclosure. Bibliographic information of the German National Library: The German National Library lists this publication in the Deutsche Nationalbibliography; Detailed bibliographic data are available on the Internet at http://dnb.d-nb.de

Table of Contents

INTRODUCTION 4

THE BUSINESSMAN 6

SECRET IN THE FOREST 13

FAST CAR 27

ALL GOOD THINGS COME IN THREES 37

TOO LONG WITHOUT SEX 43

LONG TIME NO SEE...49

SATURDAY EVENING WITH A DIFFERENCE 62

FALSE ALARM...65

Introduction

Have you ever heard of Bibliotherapy? Many ladies have practiced it for years, but few know this term.

Bibliotherapy is an academic term used to describe the amazingly beneficial (and very sexy!) thought and or body reactions that occur when reading erotic stories. In fact, sex therapists advise their female patients to read erotic stories!

Studies show that 30 to 45 minutes of reading erotic stories or sex stories cause a chemical reaction in the female brain, leading to increased arousal.

Reading sensational romantic erotic and sex stories engages the entire body, mind and soul. It puts sex at the center!

You will soon forget your role as a mother, wife, employer, or employee, and transform yourself into your sexy, seductive, and adventurous self.

Reading a satisfying love scene awakens a woman's feelings that are directly related to her libido. That's why we have some sex stories here to create for you a zone for pleasure.

Erotic reading is an excellent way to let the sensual and seductive thoughts flow. It brings sex directly into your brain and gives your imagination a sensual boost.

It's perfect for getting in the mood before sex (with yourself or your partner).

Relax your hips. Relax your stomach. Inhale.

So that you may enjoy the experience fully. Whether you are soft and tender or intense, the following stories will surely satisfy you.

Have fun while reading!

The Businessman

After spending the day drinking vodka by the pool, Maria returned to her hotel room, only to find that she was locked out. A cleaning lady looked at her suspiciously as she walked along the corridors wearing nothing but her bikini and a wet towel.

Finally she remembered that Stefan was on the same floor. She went to his room and knocked desperately on his door. After a few minutes, Stefan stuck his head out and saw her standing there, trembling, her hair still wet.

"I think I lost my room key. " said Maria

He invited her in kindly. His room was dimly lit, and parts of a newspaper were scattered on the floor. He handed her a bathrobe.

"I will make you a cup of tea". He said.

She put on the bathrobe and sat down at the small desk near the window. "Wow, your view is so much better than mine."

He chuckled. "You can come over whenever you want."

"You're such a gentleman," she said. "I'm sorry about all this."

"Not at all, I actually hoped for some company."

There was a brief silence as he poured hot water into the teacup. She admired his figure as he did that. He wore a black polo shirt with khakis and stood barefoot on the carpet. Maria had always considered him the sexiest guy in the office. He was cultured, quiet and engaging. The two had a very passionate embrace at the office Christmas party last year, and she sometimes wondered about his relationship status.

"I hope you like green tea," he said with a dimple.

"A lot!"

He sat down at the desk. "So, Maria, how do you like New York?"

They talked, laughed and flirted for an hour. Stefan played 80s pop music from his cellphone. Maria whirled out of the bathroom and the white robe floated like a cape behind her. The lights of a nearby bridge shimmered through the window.

Stefan drank whiskey from a wine glass. "I love your hair when they're curly," he finally said.

She covered her face with her hands. "Really? I think it looks stupid on me.

"No, not at all," he said, rolling the ice cubes in his glass. "Straight hair is so ... boring."

"Well, we're not in the office right now, so I think we can do what we want."

There was a smiling silence that hung between them for a moment, and Stefan put his hand on her hip. She leaned forward and kissed him in the light of the lamp. His lips were sweet with the taste of whiskey.

The kiss was incredible. The bathrobe parted as their tongues touched. She felt his grip on her hips; his touch was firm but restrained. After a few minutes, she took his hand and led him to the couch.

The couch was small and covered in floral patterns.

Stefan sat down, but Maria stopped. She pulled off the bathrobe shyly, her blue string bikini was now dry. Stefan leaned back and she noticed the contour of his swelling cock in his khakis. She leaned over him and put her hands on his legs so that her breasts dangled in front of his face. She kissed him and said, "I'm dry now ... but you'll wet me again."

Stefan grinned and closed his eyes as she reached for his pants. She carefully released the button and tugged at the waist. He wore boxer shorts in tartan pattern with his dick peeking out. She climbed on him slowly and wrapped her arms around his shoulders.

They continued to kiss violently with sensual moans. Maria grinned as he ran his fingers on her shapely ass. She untied the strings of her bikini top. She threw it across the room to revealed her breasts.

Stefan took her nipple in his mouth. Maria stuck her head back. He licked the nipple lightly. She could feel her bikini bottoms wet again. She slipped his boxer shorts awkwardly; his cock sprang out and she took him in the hand. Its circumference was impressive, and Maria's hand looked small as she pulled it up and down.

"You like touching my cock?"

"I do," she said in a timid whisper. "It's so big."

They kissed again, and she crawled over him to the other side of the couch. Stefan took her ankles and pulled her curvy hips closer. She looked at him curiously. He tore open the bikini. Maria smiled.

Stefan started to touch Maria's crotch. She had a small, dark tuft of hair. He liked it. He brushed off her shiny lips and broke them apart like the pages of a newspaper. He took it in his mouth and stroked his dark hair.

"Oh damn!" She groaned.

Her ankles were shaking. He held a hand to the inside of her thigh and squeezed her breast with the other. Her breast was still wet from his saliva and he gently licked the edges of her nipple.

Maria stared at him. She held his hair with her fingers. It was almost too much.

"Do you have a condom?" she asked.

"Can we focus on you for a while?" he answered.

Maria was not used to being cared for so much. There was almost never a starter to the main course. But Stefan did not let up. He licked her clit. Watching her in this state let all the blood run into his cock. He licked and kept playing until she finally exploded in his mouth. He had enjoyed it very much.

Stefan went to the bathroom and returned with a condom. He seemed to be holding his dick in his hand as if it were a dangerous weapon. She felt him knock a few times against her splayed bud, which glittered in the lamplight. She felt his cock slide out for a while before he put his penis in her.

"Tell me, if it hurts," he said. She nodded and felt his fingers on her hip.

It was like a dream. Their bodies moved together in a timeless rhythm. Slowly he loosened all his glory in her. Her skin shone with all the sweat on it.

"Fuck, Stefan, it's so good, fuck me deeper," she ordered.

She felt the clapping of his hand against her ass. She lowered her left leg until she felt the carpet on her bare foot.

"Oh God". Her tits swung back and forth as she screamed.

She came again. A second time. Together with him. Her back was crooked. She screamed until she had no voice left.

Maria turned and looked at Stefan. He took off the condom. She squeezed her tits together and he sprayed on her. She felt his warm, white cum falling generously over her chest. She liked that much more than she expected.

They stayed on the couch for a while.

"Shit," said Maria. "I cannot stop smiling." Then they showered together.

He gave her a big T-shirt, and she slid in bed and turned on the TV. Stefan handed her the menu. "Okay, pretty lady, time for room service."

In the next few chapters, I'd like to split the whole thing into smaller pieces to make it easier and more helpful to grasp.

Secret in the forest

The incoming message buzzes in my pocket. I pull out my phone and look at the screen.

"Meet me in 20 minutes! Our place!"

I bite my lip. It's a terrible time. I am working on a file for an early morning meeting and I should really finish it now, not in two hours.

I stop for a moment and think. The phone is humming again in my hand with a second message.

"Please, baby, I need you."

Well, it always is. My weakness. Any combination of words with "baby" and "need" and I'm on my way.

I keep telling myself that I'll stop, but he knows how to press my buttons. And who am I fooling here? I love it when he presses my buttons.

I close my laptop, run my fingers through my hair, and put on my boots. I stop at the door with the keys already in my hand and yell back in the flat to my roommate.

"I have to go buy some things," I say. "Do you want something?"

"Nope."

"Cool, see you later," I say. The door closes behind me before the words even make it out of my mouth.

I get in my car as fast as possible and start driving.

"What are you doing?" I say softly as I drive around. "Last time should have been the last time, remember?"

I sigh. Now I'm talking to myself. I'm going downhill, I think.

"Alright, the last time, but really, definitely this is the last time, that's so bad, that bad."

I turn on the radio to keep from these thoughts.

Ten minutes later I drive through an industrial park and finally arrive in a residential area. I turn left, then right and finally left again until I am there and park in the light of a single street lamp. On my right, a forest; to my left, a row of new houses.

Only two or three are inhabited from their appearance. "For Sale" signboards stand in front of two of the dark houses and those with the lights on have their curtains closed.

Nobody can see me, I say to myself. I grab my phone and send a short message: "I just parked. I'll be right there. "

I jump out of the car and go into the woods. For a moment, I see my shadow spreading in front of me as I walk on the path, but in a few seconds the streetlights are blocked by the trees. I have no shade left now, and it's so dark that I can barely see my own feet while my eyes slowly adjust.

I turn on the light of my phone and set it down so I do not take a wrong step.

I look at my phone. Still, no answer. When I turn the torch back on my feet, I finally see what I'm looking for: a little light coming towards me.

It's him.

He stands at the other end of the forest and comes from the opposite direction as me. This is our "job" and when I think about things we've done here, I get a little bit upset.

Of course, the last time was not the last time. How could it be? This dark place, this safe shaded place where nobody can see us - how could I want to be anywhere else?

I stop walking and let him come to me. The light is getting closer and closer and closer until it's still a few steps away from me. The light goes out and I can only see his shape. A dark shadow.

He finds me in the dark, stretches his hands, hugs me and puts his head on my neck. I hear him breathe deeply.

"Oh damn, baby," he says. "I damned missed you. I've missed you so. "

He grabs me tight and pulls me to him. His hands roll over my back to grab my butt and squeeze it hard.

"Come here," he says, reaching for my hand and turning his small flashlight back on.

We leave the path and move sideways into the forest. He moves left and right and ducks under low branches until we come across a small clearing. There is a bit more light here, as the trees have less foliage, so the moonlight reflects on our faces.

"Can't we do this more often? I want more, I want it every day, not just here, but ... you know ... everywhere," he says.

I shake my head.

"No. You know we cannot."

"Why? What if I just invite you to dinner - and we just go? Why is that so complicated? "

"No. "

"But I want you."

"You have me, here, right now."

To keep him from talking, I start to touch him. I put my hand on his chest and find his nipple.

He may know how to press my buttons, but I also know how to press his buttons.

He stretches his head to the back.

"Fuck, baby ... I ... I think we should ... Oh God, shit," he gasps, as my other hand reaches the other nipple.

He's breathing harder now and I drop my other hand to the front of his pants.

Rock hard, taut against his zipper. I run my fingers over it and hear him breathe again as he pushes his hips forward.

"Did you say something?" I asked.

He cannot even answer.

I love to know that I can do that to him. I love to know that he will play this moment later in his head and will be so excited that he has to bring himself back to orgasm. I love knowing that he goes to bed as soon as he comes home without taking a shower, so the smell of me is still with him when he wakes up.

I kneel down in front of him and take off his pants.

"Oh God, fuck, .. fuck," he says, the stream of words that repeat themselves in his agitation over and over again.

I pull down my pants and put my hands on his hips. He is trembling now, but not because of the cold.

"I need you," he says.

"Not yet," I say.

I take his cock in my hand and stroke it gently. He moans and I feel that he is getting harder and thicker in my hand. My other hand reaches down, takes his eggs and presses lightly.

"Fuck!" He yells.

"Shhhhh," I answer.

He looks down at me. I know there's just enough light for him to see the contours of my face and the swinging of my hair as I waver in front of him. I slowly open my mouth and look at him all the time. I let my tongue slowly slide out again. And then I let my tongue slide over the shaft of his cock as I feel and taste it. If I think he cannot bear it anymore, I'll take him in my mouth and close my lips, suck him as deeply as possible.

His hands then fall on my head, fingers in my hair. I move my hands to his hips. I feel like my panty gets wet. He moves in, pushing himself slowly into my mouth and I'm suddenly desperate because I wish he had his hard cock in me.

I moan, a deep, deep sound that undoubtedly vibrates through his penis. The first groaning is coincidental, but the second one, I do on purpose, because I know that it will make him crazy. He pulls his cock out of my mouth, grabs my shoulders and pulls me to him.

"I have to fuck you, now."

There is no room for discussion in his tone.

"The tree trunk," I say, looking to the left.

He takes off his jacket and throws it over the tree trunk. I get on my knees and put my chest over the tree trunk. My breasts, still in my bra under my shirt, slide against his coat.

I feel him moving behind me and his hands caressing my back.

When he is at waist level, his warm fingers slip under my pants and he pulls it down as far as he can. He pushes my top up to my shoulders.

He kisses my back and I feel his grip on my buttocks. His warm tongue is on my butt, then on my bud. Once he has tasted me, he moans and licks harder.

"Ohhh, fuck, fuck, shit!"

I am incapable of real words. Just "fuck" over and over again, as his tongue penetrates down over my stomach, my clit right up to my vagina.

Oh, it's so good, shit!

Again, he licks my butt with his tongue and suddenly I feel his thumb as he licks the moisture left behind by his tongue. Up and down and pushes his thumb into my anus. I'm panting. He has never done that. It feels so good, that I catch myself bumping into his hand.

"Do you like that?"

"Yes, shit, yes ...."

"Next time, my cock?"

"Oh ... oh god ... oh my god ..." I cannot say yes or no. The idea is so exciting that I wish I could ask for it now.

But just then I feel his hard cock press against my pussy. He rubs his stiff cock a few times and looks for the right place. When he finds it, he pushes his full glory into me. His thumb is still in my butt. And his cock penetrates further and further into my pussy. I feel as he pleasures me from both sides, feel his thumb and his stiff, hard member, both as they penetrate into me at the same time.

"Oh ... Fuck yes, YES, hardener, please, shit!"

He does not need to be asked again: his thumb slips deeper and his cock goes even deeper into my pussy. His free hand lets my hip loose and I feel him let go. Then a clap. I realise that he hit me on the cheek. He has never done that either.

"Again," I moan.

"God, I love to do that to you," I hear him whisper. His voice fidgets.

We continue in the dark and move in despair against each other. After a while I feel his hand firmly on my hip for a moment. Again he raises his hand. A third blow, and a fourth, and I feel the hard cumshot. Then he moans, his body trembling as he squirts.

He goes down with his lips to kiss my back as he bends over me and thrusts deep into me one last time.

When his orgasm ends, he pulls out his penis, it's only half-stiff. His sperm runs out of my vagina, over a thigh. "Here's a handkerchief," he says. I wipe it off and thank him.

"Will you please go out to dinner with me?" He suddenly asks me.

"No."

"Come on!"

I move away from him, get up and put my clothes back on. I lean on him, kiss his mouth and smile.

"I cannot, I have a big case, I'll probably have to work a lot."

"But you're the boss," he says.

"Yes. That means I have to work a lot. No dinner."

"Can we eat in the conference room?"

"Will you consider it as a date?" I ask.

"Well," he says. "Maybe. Yes. Do you want?"

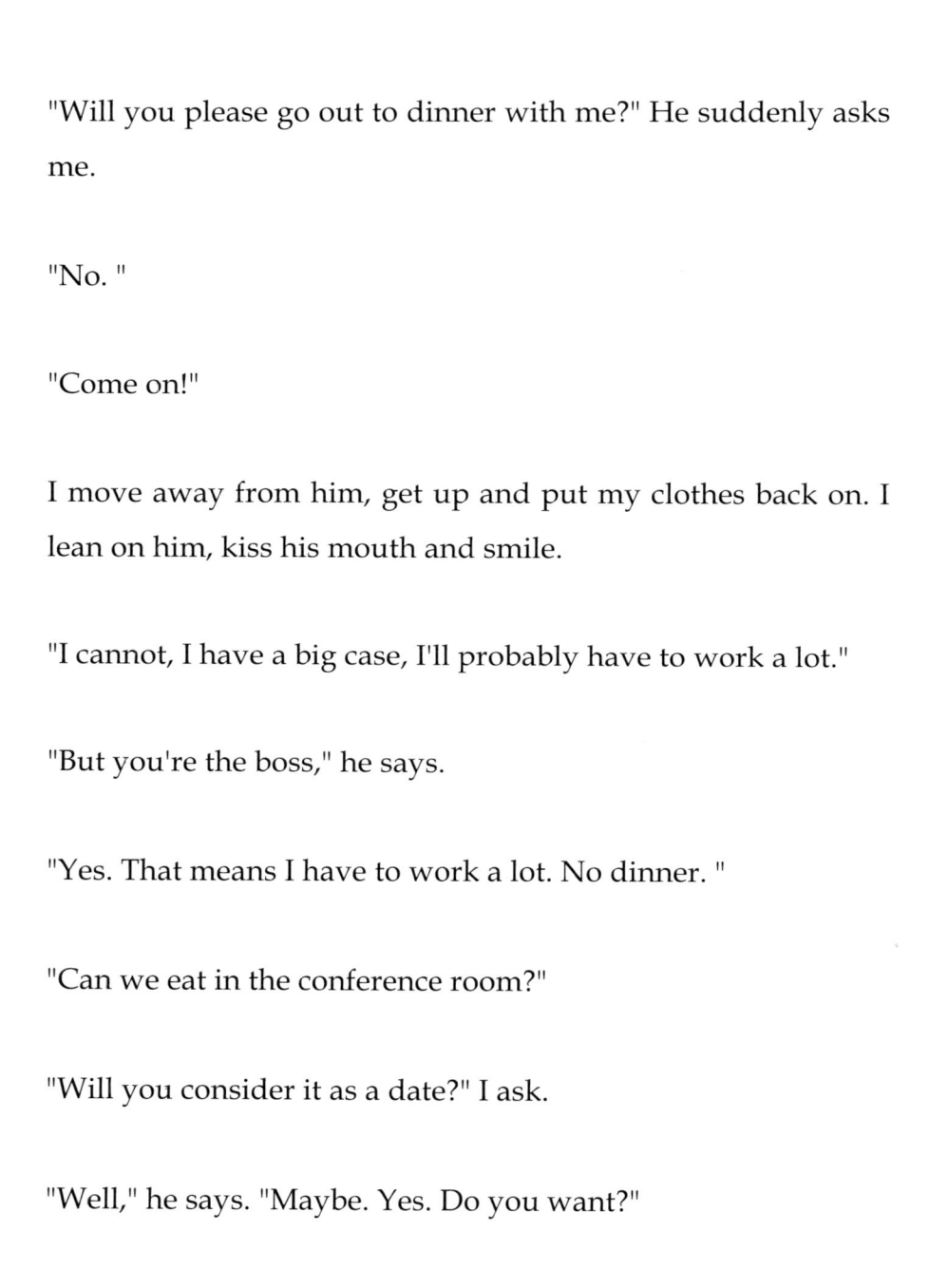

"Good," I say, laughing. "I cannot go out with my staff, remember?"

I go back to the car and he follows me. Once again, he hits me on my ass.

"Well," he says, "Maybe you should promote me. And then you will not be my boss anymore. "

"I own the whole company, I'll always be your boss."

"Good. But will you meet me next week? "

I sigh. "Maybe. No promises. "

"I'll do the thing with my thumb again," he says.

We have reached the path by which we separate; Time for me to go right and for him to go left.

"What thing?" I ask casually.

"You know exactly," he says with a laugh.

"Maybe I'll meet you next week, let's see how my staff deal with this case, I'm sure hard work ... will be rewarded."

"You're terrible," he says laughing.

"Yes."

He kisses me again, puts his arms around me and leans against my ear.

"Thanks for fucking, boss, see you tomorrow morning."

He drops his hands, puts them on my buttocks and pushes them.

"See you in the morning," I answer.

Fast Car

I bang his door shut and turn the key before I close the car door and buckle up. I know it's over this time. Forever. Gary is a fucking asshole and I'm pretty sure his mother called him Garrett. An idiotic name for an idiot man. Boys, I mean. Definitely boy, not a man.

Yes, it was almost like the cliché scene where the woman enters her boyfriend's apartment, suspicious but still cautious. She is not sure yet. She turns her key into the lock and shouts "Hello," slowly sneaks into his bedroom and opens the door. And, of course, there he is, with his cock deep in the pussy of a small blonde, too young, without any body hair or blemish. The kind of girls you can see on "teen" porn sites.

I drive fast down the highway in the July afternoon heat. My red, short jeans shorts slip while I drive. I'm not sure where I'm going because I've just been evicted from my own flat where I should move in with him. Yes, that was the plan. I mean, I had boxes in my car and had packed everything. Ready to move in with him.

With a car full of boxes and a full heart of rage I'm looking for something other than answers. Because deep inside of me, I knew it all along and still got into this nonsense and maybe, just maybe because I did not love myself the way I should. I am sick.

I ought to know better than riding full speed at 180km / h on the highway now. I'm 30 years old, for heaven's sake. Suddenly I see a blue light in the rearview mirror. "Oh, no, that's all I need!" I sigh.

A policeman on his motorcycle chases me and asks me to drive right.

This cop, looks like he eats a girl like me for breakfast. My head falls on the steering wheel as he approaches the car. I cannot afford this now. I pull my tight white top a little lower. Not that my breasts are big enough to have a cleavage or something, but skin is skin, right? And my shorts do everything else. I stop and let my window down.

"How fast was I officer?" I look at him sheepishly.

"Driver's license and vehicle registration papers, please, Ma'am."

"I give them to him. "Ma'am, do you know that you drove 60km/h above the top speed?"

"Did I really?" I do my best to sound horrified, I'm really a pretty good actress. "I'm so sorry, sir, I understand this is unacceptable, it's just ..."

For a fraction of a second, I think about what kind of lie best suits the occasion. What would make this tall, white, blonde, green-eyed policeman to empathize with me? I quickly scan the man: he is well built. Good-looking for a policeman. Damn it. No wedding ring. He's probably 38, 39. His badge says Donovan.

"Officer Donovan, as you can see I have here, a car full of boxes."

Calling him by the name distracts him from writing for 3 seconds. He looks down at me, a subtle grin on his tanned face.

I continue. "I was on my way to my boyfriend's. I was to move in with him. We wanted to get married and everything, "I lie." And, when I arrived and was unloading my boxes, I walked into our bedroom to find him with another woman. "He looks at me more keenly now, despite everything, I start to cry.

"Officer, I know it's no excuse, but I was just so upset and I did not know what to do or where to go. Please have some pity and tuen a blind eye to the traffic fines and penalties. I really can't afford it now and this is my first citation for driving too fast. I promise it will not happen again." I wipe the tears with my hand and look up to him for the first time since I began crying. He has stopped writing and is staring at me very carefully. He slowly pulls out a handkerchief from his pocket and gives it to me.

"Ma'am," he says softly. "I'm sorry to hear it all. For real. I have experienced something like this myself, so I can sympathize with you. "

He hesitates a bit. No other soul is on this deserted road. "I hope it's ok to address you informally," he says to me cautiously.

"Okay, look, I've never done this before because I do not believe in exceptions, but I can see that you're really hurt and some of us policemen have a heart." He smiles, damn, he's really sexy, and he does not look like he wants to kill me anymore, that's a good sign!

"Look, consider this your lucky day, okay, I'll overlook this time and forget the ticket, okay, my dear, but never let me catch you racing on these roads again, or you'll have to pay the next time, okay? "The corners of his mouth resisted a big smile, but I could see it anyway.

"Oh my God! Really? Thank you, Officer, I cannot thank you enough, I really can't."

"You're welcome." He looks at me- my long black hair. My white top, low enough for him to see everything he needs to see. I am not wearing a bra. I'm cute enough to get away with it. I can feel his eyes resting there. And then down to my shorts which, I admit, look more like underwear.

"What is your name?" He asks.

"Um, er, Ella".

"Ella, I can see it on your driver's license," he chuckles and hands it back to me. "Nice name."

"Thanks." I'm sweating.

"Ella, I realize this is something outrageous, even unprofessional, but, er, can I invite you to dinner someday?"

Later that night, after drowning some of my worries in a bottle of rum and then getting sober again, I find myself at the policeman's front door. I managed to take a shower in my friend Erika's house, and I am wearing a flattering little flower dress that is tight at the top, loose and short at the bottom. He makes dinner for me and I find the turn of events very amusing.

While I'm sitting there watching him finish the tasty steaks and the delicious Greek salad, we go over small talk. His wife left him for another man two years ago. His twelve-year-old daughter lives with her mother. But what was really interesting was his ass in those perfect khakis. My God, I watched the thing in the kitchen move back and forth as there was nothing else to admire in his single apartment.

I sneak up behind him and somehow hug him around his ass. He drops the knife and takes a deep breath as he throws his head back. Good reaction.

"How about ... a starter before we eat?" I say.

"Mmm. Yes ... I think that's a good idea, "he says.

He turns and my legs bump on his hips. My flip-flops fall off my feet. He puts his two hands on my buttocks, he leans forward and we kiss each other. The man is an incredible kisser.

He bites me on my lower lip. He carries me into the bedroom and drops me onto the bed. He leaves the room and comes back with his handcuffs. My heart is jumping.

"Is that okay?" He asks with a grin. "I mean, I let you get away somehow. I would feel better about the whole thing if I could punish you in another way. "

"Yes," I say. "Yes." I never told my friends, but it was always one of my fantasies to get fucked by a cop.

"Good girl," he grumbles softly, half lying on top of me to clamp my wrists on his bedposts. The metal feels cold on my burning skin. Then, to my surprise, he kneels over me, he takes my dress from above and tears it open. No kidding, the buttons fly everywhere in the room. Our eyes close.

He gets up and undresses. A pretty tall man stands in front of me, hairy and muscular. In his black boxer shorts, I can see how his cock moves. Oh damn, his cock is huge. My underwear seems to drive him crazy. He takes a deep breath as he pulls it off and throws it behind him. He pulls out two hidden restraints under the mattress to keep my ankles in place: My legs are wide open. Now I am completely at his mercy and I enjoy every moment. The steak smells great, waiting in the other room. But my mouth is watering because of him.

He leaves the room again and comes back this time with his baton: black and hard.

He lays it gently over my mouth, my lips until I open it and start to suck it. Slowly and then harder as he pushes the rod deep into my mouth. Who knew that sucking this thing can feel so good?

"Do you like that, Ella?" He asks, taking it out of my mouth.

"Yes," I gasp.

"Good. "

Then he pushes the rod into the center of my chest, first one and then the other breast and rotates it, in order to create a weak burn..

"Ohhh ... you know how to use this thing, right?"

He smiles and holds his fingers to my lips. "Shhh. "He continues and slides it up to my vagina.

He pushes his staff with its not now glittering tip. Only a few centimeters. Oh my God. It's so hard that I'm forced to relax all my muscles so as not to resist.

He pulls the stick out again, shoves it back in and massages me in my pleasure temple, pointing slightly up to meet my G spot. I've never been so excited in my life. He shoves the hard stick back into me as if it were his own dick. My hips are lifting, my head is deep in the pillow and I scream out loudly. He pulls the stick out again, strokes and gently kisses my Venus cave.

"Mmmm. That was a delicious appetizer. Are you ready for a steak? "He asks laughing while holding his cock.

"Why don't you come first?" I say.

"Let's save that for dessert," he says. "This meal has many courses."

"All right," I say.

Maybe my luck changes, as well as my dumb taste in men.

At least I think I'm now ready to tell my friends about my fantasy.

All Good Things Come In Threes

"I just want him to notice me." She wanted it so much. The girl crept into a big empty office. She liked this office. Her boss looked so hot in that chair. Every time she saw him, she got wet, she wanted to fuck him so much. But as much as she wanted it, he did not pay attention to her and she did not like it, so she made provocative videos and emailed them.

She was sure the building was closed and she made herself as comfortable as possible. She set the tripod in front of a huge desk and started the video.

Someone opened the door and went into the hallway.

Some strange noises came from his office. He kept listening. "What the hell? Moaning? Who's this who is not afraid to fuck in his office? He did not want to scare anyone, so he opened the door quietly and very lightly. The scene that followed was magical.

One of his employees lay on his favorite table masturbating. Who was she and why did she do it?

He just had sex, but this scene turned him on right away. He came closer. It was that very hot chick he saw on the first day. The first thought that came to his mind was "How does her vagina taste?" And he could not get that thought out of his head. He pretended he did not want her ... but it was not true. He took another step closer. Her legs are wide open, the pussy moist and shiny and her fingers playing with it. Then he saw the camera and the tripod.

"Naughty girl, making a video for someone?" He turned off the camera.

Well, what have we here? He took a big chair and sat down in front of her spread-out legs, admiring her wet pussy. The girl was frightened and fell to the floor, quickly moving to the other end of the desk.

"Oh my God, I'm so sorry, I ... I did not think there was anyone here." She covered her crotch with her hand. "I'll be gone in a minute, I'm so sorry."

"You think I'll believe you did not stage it. You recorded your lust game with this camera, I'll check it out later."

She searched desperately for her skirt. She had no panties. She had to get out of here.

"I do not care, ... I have to go. Excuse, please."

"Do not move, you're not going anywhere, I'm not sure you're done, I cannot let you go if you're not done yet."

"I do not think I can do it now. And I need something ... bigger than my fingers and ... thicker."

"I'm sure I have something for you. Come here." He lifted her skirt from the floor.

"Umm, just give me my skirt and I'll go. You've never noticed me anyway, so, I'm not sure that you are not gay."

"I'll show you what a gay man I am. I warn you for the last time, come here."

She looked at the distance between him and the door, thinking she had a chance to escape. Like a frightened animal she went to the window and reached the door. She pulled on the door handle. "Locked."

She suddenly felt strong hands on her waist. He turned her over and pushed her against the wall.

"Hold on to the wall."

"No, wait, what are you doing, stop?"

"I said, hold on to the damned wall, you'll need it."

He picked her up until her vagina reached his mouth. "I bet you taste fantastic."

She had no choice but to follow his wish. She put her legs on his shoulders. He began to lick her wet vagina with his mouth and slid his tongue directly into her dripping vagina. The emotions were so strong that she had no choice but to grab the wall and moan deeply. God, he did it so intensely. She felt his tongue licking her juices. Gravity did its best and she could barely move.

She had no chance to escape his swirling and magical tongue. She screamed until she finally came to orgasm. He did not stop. He had shifted all his attention to her vagina and to the throbbing clit. He sucked his lips ... he wanted a second orgasm. She tasted so good. She scratched his chest with her nails. "Oh my god, I .... fuck!" She could not say anything. Now he was penetrating her with his hard, stiff cock.

"I want you to come."

"No, please, I cannot, it's too much."

"Relax, I'm a big boy."

She was so wet that she felt no pain, but the feeling was so crazy. Every muscle of her vagina stretched enough to give her true pleasure. She had experienced what it feels like to have two such strong orgasms in just 5 minutes.

Now he pushed his thick cock into me. His cock was so big and reached all parts of my dripping hole. I almost howled, it was so good. He fucked me gently but deeply, giving me time to adjust to the size of his cock. When I got wet enough, he fucked me harder and harder until he came in me.

My tight vagina pressed all the juice from his cock. It was a hot and delicate torture at the same time. He leaned over to my ear and whispered in a low voice "I thought it was very nice and I want to fuck you again! Next time you come directly to me or call me if you want to be pampered! ".

He pulled out his half-stiff cock, gave me my underwear and my skirt, we got dressed and left the office one by one.

Too Long Without Sex

I am a single mother and I haven't had sex for over 2 years. I am a single mother and a teacher.

My boyfriend dumped me when our child was two years old. My little boy is almost five now and I have hardly had any dates during that time. Either no time or no desire for a date.

When I see an attractive guy, I get turned on in seconds. So, I have not had normal sex for more than two years. My best "lover" is my vibrating "John". Do not ask me why "John". I just like the name. That has been my only sex partner, the vibrating John.

Every two weeks, I meet with the parents of my students to talk about their children and their achievements. I love these kids, but I love their parents even more. Especially the fathers, who sometimes, arouse me deeply that I let my imagination play.

That evening, when I was about to go home, somebody suddenly knocked on the door. "Come in," I said. The door opened cautiously and I was pleasantly shocked. Here he was, the hero of my fantasies. I did not know who he was, but he looked so good - tall, athletically built man. Under his dark brown silky shirt, one could see lines of his well-trained muscles.

"I'm sorry if I interrupted you, I'm looking for Ms. Wicht."

"It's me." I took a deep breath and tried not to stare at him too much. The handsome man came to me and shook my hand.

"Hello my name is David, I'm Henry's dad."

His hand was so warm and strong. I tried not to look at him. My brain started drawing bad images.

"Yes, David, I was just getting ready to leave. How can I help you? It's a bit late and I have to go home."

"It will only take a few minutes. I was wondering about one thing."

"Yes, what?"

I took my purse and started walking to the door.

"Is it possible for my son to get an A in the next test?"

I stopped in the middle of the way to the door.

"Excuse me, so you want me to put my reputation on the line so that your kid gets a good grade?"

"I'll do what's necessary ... and even more," his eyes looked at me slowly.

"David, I do not think it's a good idea, I'm sure I cannot do that."

I was nervous. I knew what he was offering and I wanted it so much. I felt my bud wriggle. Oh, it wanted his big cock so much.

"Think again, are you sure I cannot do anything for you, I'm pretty sure you taste pretty damn good, and my tongue wants to give you some pleasure."

My whole body became stiff when he spoke of his tongue. I could swear that I almost had an orgasm after his dirty words.

"I have to go. Excuse me!"

I held tightly to my purse and walked on to the door. Suddenly, I felt his strong arms around my waist. A movement and he pushed me to the wall next to the door. He threw my purse aside and raised my arms over my head.

"David, please, let me go. Anyone can walk in at any moment. We just cannot". "Pssst," he closed my mouth with his finger.

"I know you want it. I can feel it."

"But ... "

"No but, just enjoy it. "

He took off my skirt and tore open my panties. I was already so wet by fantasies. He dropped to his knees and began to pamper me. I was so horny. It was not long before I came in his mouth. He did not stop. I stretched my legs wider and he licked so deeply. I felt two fingers in me and they rubbed gently in my vagina. God, he was so good.

"I'll eat your mound down to the last drop, you taste so great."

He took off his shirt. His muscles were so sexy. His tongue torturing my vagina. I wanted to feel his cock so much in me.

"Please, fuck me," I touched my nipples. He took off his pants slowly. A big and thick cock was in front of me. Now it was my turn. I went to my knees and covered this "beauty" with my mouth. He groaned deeply. I started to lick his stiff splendor like an ice cream and wanted to have everything in my mouth at once. Oh, dear sir, he was so tall. My tongue licked the tip and played with the hole. I have not licked a big cock for a long time. He stopped me and licked my pussy further.

"I need it so much, please"

He was about to go with his cock in my wet vagina.

"Not yet," he held up my hands again. He played with his big boy and tried to gather strength. Then, a quick and deep movement and I groaned.

"Please do not stop. "

The movements became faster and deeper.

"Promise me you will do what I want, or I will not let you come." It felt so good, I would sell my soul to the devil.

"Yes, I will do what you want, just keep going."

His strong arms held my butt. He got deeper with each movement. He did not stop and fucked me on. I moved my hips faster and faster until I reached orgasm. I almost lost my mind - it felt so good.

Now I did not want to return to my "John", so I had to do my homework and find a guy to fuck. Or win over this guy for me to spend more hot hours with.

Long Time No See

"Shit, shit, shit, OK, do not worry, just relax," Amy thought in her parked car, her hands on the wheel. "Everyone's nervous at class reunions."

After one last look in the mirror, she undid her seat belt and took a deep breath and stepped out into the evening air.

She went to the school she had completed ten years ago. It felt like a half-forgotten dream: everything felt somehow familiar, but also alien. She had no time to remember. She had decided to be late to give everyone else a chance to drink a little and skip the initial embarrassment, but she was already far too late.

She entered the reception area and followed the instructions glued to the walls of the building, looking at all the small changes. She had not really known what to expect, so she had done her best not to do too much or too little. She had done well, she guessed. Formal, informal, in a black pencil skirt and a black, open top. A subtle silver chain. Hair long and straight.

She stepped into the gym and through an archway with "Welcome Class '06" in glittering neon letters. The room was full of people and every face was familiar to her in one way or another. She stood under a colorful arc and everyone remembered long-forgotten anecdotes, stories and relationships. She had not had contact with the majority of these people for a decade, and yet she felt like she'd never been away.

Just when it felt a bit overwhelming, a voice came over the humming of the conversation and the background of the deliberately ironic music of 2006.

"Amy! AMY!" The voice called.

Amy turned to see Sara, her old study partner and organizer of the event, who came to Amy with two glasses of champagne.

"Hey, how are you?"

"Sara!" Amy replied as she took the glass and clasped it awkwardly.

"I'm fine, very good, very strange, to be here again," she said, looking around the room.

"Where have you been? We have not heard much from you over the years," Sara asked.

"Well, I traveled for a couple of years, got a job overseas, just returned home for a job a year ago, I got into the real estate business," Amy replied, suddenly realizing how hard it is to live ten years in one single sentence.

Wow, great, that sounds so exciting, you look awesome, "Sara said.

Amy was totally happy to be here in school. She was in a good mood, but not particularly interested in guys or their looks. Apart from one. Sam, the guy she'd lost her virginity to ten years ago.

The memory was triggered by Sara's compliment. Sam had been following her for weeks. Amy knew he liked her, she did not really know why, but she did not care, because she did not really like him. It was not personal: she just did not like anyone that way. But what she found out was that Sam did not. He was not remarkably handsome, and he was the guy who did not look good. Amy and Sam had a common interest, namely mutual disinterest.

That was all it was. Finally, simply out of perseverance, Sam won her and they started spending time together. It was at the end of the last year, close to graduation. They both suspected that they would never meet again and thought that they should at least have sex, right? None of them had done it before and this could be their last chance.

And they did it. It was so embarrassing, fiddly, funny and fast, as you can imagine from the first time. Since then, they have never met again. Sam went to college and Amy went traveling.

Amy had come a long way since high school. She was a good student, but always in the background. There were only a few people in this class reunion who were in a hurry to talk to her. But now, as she looked around, she realized that all the travels she had done, all the success, the sun she had seen, all the clean air she breathed, and the fresh food she ate had been better than this.

At that moment of her unexpected pride, she suddenly heard another voice.

"Amy?" He said.

Amy turned to the voice. It was Sam. Of course he was.

"Holy shit, what are the chances that you will be the first person I meet?" Sam asked with a big smile.

"Sam, I was literally thinking of you," she replied, looking at each other for several seconds.

"Um, I'll be back later," Sara said, politely aware of the moment that passed before her, and she backed away into the crowd.

"Oh, that's cute," Sam said. "I still think of you sometimes. Crazy how quickly people lose touch after high school, eh? "

"I think so. I wanted it, to be honest. I do not know. I was young, I just wanted to break the link with my teen and get on with things as soon as possible, I do not really know why.

It is really nice to see you, how are you? "Amy asked, suddenly realizing that she had accidentally offended Sam.

"I'm fine and I understand what you mean," Sam answered to her relief. "I feel a little uncomfortable being here again. I'm so late because I could not even decide if I should come or not, you know? And now I'm here, it's not really real. It's like, I do not know, experiencing someone else's memories or something like that. "

"Deep, Maaan," Amy nudged.

Sam bowed his head and smiled a little sheepishly.

"I suddenly feel so old," Sam said and changed the subject skillfully.

You do not look like it. You look good. You've really grown up, haven't you? "Amy said.

After college, he became a photographer and saw a lot of the world, as did Amy. He was brown-tanned, slender and a lot more muscular than when they last met.

"Ah," he said modestly, "thank you. I usually look like I slept in a barn. This evening I'm wearing a shirt. This is my effort for tonight. This shirt."

"You try too hard, you should just take it off"

"It's a school meeting," he answered. "Nobody here needs to be reunited with my nipples."

"No," Amy said. "The nipple reunion is next week."

"I'll definitely come to that," Sam said. "I could even arrive early. Bad social events are always better without a shirt. But only as long as everyone is present is without. If there are 50 people and only two nipples, it is especially embarrassing for everyone. But if there are 50 people and 100 nipples, that's a party. "

"That's where you can make good use of your college education," Amy said.

"I honestly do not know what the hell I'm talking about," Sam laughed.

"Me neither," Amy replied, "but it's probably the most interesting conversation I'll have tonight. Should we just disappear? There are not many people I wanted to see. "

Sam pretended to think. "Well, I was hoping to meet someone who is a lawyer. It is always good to have a lawyer as a friend. But yes, let's go. "

Somehow, they both knew what would happen next. A kind of unconscious agreement. They had continued exactly where they had left after school, with the same slow chemistry that defined their relationship. But this time there was something else. They shared a little more maturity, a little more experience and a lot more self-confidence. This time the chemistry was not burning so slowly. And they both knew it.

They joked and kept flirting as they walked down the corridors to the parking lot when Amy noticed something. She pulled Sam to the door of a classroom and looked through the glass.

"Do you remember this room?" She asked.

Sam thought for a minute. He stepped behind her and pressed his weight against her, so he too could see through the window. Through the window, they could see a stack of tables stacked on top of each other.

"Sure ...," he said, collecting his memories. "This is the room where you finally agreed to go out with me."

Amy turned to face him, her back against the door. She slid her hand to the door handle and squeezed it. The door opened, a glow from the corridor permeating the darkness of the classroom. She put a finger in his pants, stepped back and pulled him inside. The door closed behind them, she pushed him against it and kissed him.

Sam kissed back. He had changed. She could tell by his kiss. Sam felt Amy smile at his lips. Amy felt his cock through his pants.

"Judging me?" Sam asked jokingly.

"Maybe," said Amy. "And maybe it's much better than last time."

"Let's see what else I'm better at," Sam said as he held her hips and continued to kiss her.

He pushed her back to the center of the room without taking his lips off her until her ass was on a table. Still unable to break his kiss, Sam moved his hands to her legs and began slowly pushing up Amy's skirt. He kept walking until she leaned against the desk with her legs spread, naked from the waist down to her black heels.

Sam stepped back to look at her.

"You look so damned good," he breathed, as if he could not stop the words if he wanted to.

He knelt down and he held her ankle in one hand and his ass with the other. He went with his tongue to her pussy and nestled his face in her panties. She watched him from above, her heart rate increasing. She put her slender fingers on the back of his head and pulled his face into her, lifting her hips slightly. He licked her through her panties, his eyes closed and his breath was deep and warm on her skin.

When she started to moan, Sam started to lick her vagina with his tongue. Slowly he lifts her legs onto his shoulders.

"Fuck me," she whispered down to him.

"No," he answered.

Still on his knees, he pushed her back, she lay on the desk, her knees in the air and apart, her fingers still woven in his hair.

Sam continued. He turned his head to her and he began to lick her tenderly, firmly and slowly.

But Amy was not in the mood for tenderness. She wanted him to pleasure her. She pulled his face hard against her vagina. Sam, still with his eyes closed, made Amy go crazy with his tongue. Sam's stifled moan of pleasure told Amy how good she tasted.

"Damn. Oh shit. Yes" Amy growled through clenched teeth. She noticed that Sam's whole body was shaking. She could not see, but she knew he had loosened his pants and stroked his cock. Sam's tongue went deeper into her, the moaning of his moaning wet her vagina. She moved her other hand to her clit and began stroking it in rhythm with Sam's tongue.

Her short gasps began to unite as she felt the beginning of an orgasm through her body.

"Oh shit, Sam. I am coming," she said, her eyes closed and her head arching forward, every muscle in her body tense.

"Do it. In my face," Sam growled in Amy's vagina.

Her moaning became a squeak as she stroked faster and faster and went deeper and deeper with Sam's tongue. She was close, so close. And then her body froze for a minute. Her whole body was disheveled with pleasure, it started in her hair, ran over her body and into her labia and directly on Sam's pretty, panting face.

Her hand came away from his hair and fell on her mound. Sam leaned on his heels with a smile on his wet face. It was great.

"Shit ... I did not expect that it would happen tonight."

"I did it" Sam said with a grin. "Well, I hoped. I wanted to apologize for the first time being so crappy. "

"Oh Sam, that's cute," Amy said. "You were not that bad. But you should definitely apologize more often. "

Saturday evening with a difference

Alex and I had only been together for a few weeks, only long enough to immerse ourselves in our feelings for each other. Even in public, Max could hardly keep his hands off me, and I loved annoying him when he could least use my slim and inviting figure. This became a game between us, and I took every opportunity to drive him mad with subtle touches and playful allusions.

It was Saturday night and we enjoyed a nice dinner in a restaurant serving good drinks, good food and loud music.

As we sat down and enjoyed the company, I shoved my hand under the table and pushed his cock through his pants. For a good hour, I did so while enjoying his rising but frustrated excitement.

I made him crazy and his cock throbbed under my touch. He was crazy with lust and all he could think about was to bring me home and fuck me, which I clearly wanted.

I had probably pushed him too far.

"Did you see the waitress smiling at us?" I whispered in his ear. "She knows that I play with your cock. I bet it made her almost as horny as me. "Then I chuckled and squeezed him tight. "I cannot wait to feel you in me."

I felt his heart pounding and his self-control simply stopped. With a wild grunt he kissed me hard. He dropped a handful of twenties on the table and fixed his smoldering gaze on me. "You will not have to wait long," he said as he quickly led me outside.

I started to smile as he pushed me into the backseat of his car. "What do you do! Oh my god, David! There are people there! We cannot do it here! "I said.

It's dark and nobody's going to care anyway, and you drove me crazy all night and I'm not waiting until we get home! "Said David.

"Oh God, David, I can not believe you do that!" it came over me.

I might have said no, but when he closed the door, I started kissing him. And as I wanted. We fiddled around in our clothes until his pants clenched on his knees and my skirt clenched at my waist. As he brought his throbbing erection to my soaking wet grotto of lust, my eyes widened, my breathing became irregular and I took his cock and led him inside.

He felt my wetness and pushed hard with his cock in me. I closed my eyes as he started to fuck me in the backseat. My hands gripped his shoulders and when we found our rhythm we kissed passionately.

I felt that he was already on the verge of jerking off and it only took a few minutes for him to feel the heat of orgasm in his stomach. I held on tight and hooked my legs behind him as he plunged hard into me.

"Come on, David, fuck me, fuck me hard, baby, I want to feel it!" I moan.

Moments later, his body hardened like steel and his cock was deep as it exploded inside me. It was an incredible moment and we both laughed as he climbed over the seat to get to the steering wheel.

False Alarm

Besides the characterless office, it could have been worse for Sara. But Sara did not have much time. Everything was urgent. Everything had a deadline. The office became her life. Her routine was to wake up on Monday, get dressed, eat, work, return, wash and then repeat everything.

Sara lost her spark somewhere along the way and she felt it. A vague feeling that she missed something essential. Every time she left a room, she patted imaginary bags as if she always felt she had forgotten something. This feeling was with her every moment. But it was not her keys she had forgotten. It was something much more basic than that.

But she also had fun sometimes. Now and then she would like to smoke a cigarette and wake up the rebel in her. Maybe once a month she wore something provocative under her suit, something only she could see. Her little secret. It was only a small thing, but it made her feel more brave, and she smiled a little more than usual. She had to protect this secret.

But it was not enough anymore. She had stopped counting the months since her last date, not to mention her last affair. She wondered what had happened to her. She took risks. She used to be spontaneous. She wanted to reconnect with herself and she knew it would not happen if she took no chances and allowed it.

But today she felt special. She had to open a valve and release the dangerous pressure she had built uncontrollably.

And there was Mark. Mark was new, Sara had interviewed him for the job, feeling uncomfortable when she realized she was flirting with him. Her face blushed after she accidentally said "Oh really ..." when he said he was flexible in every position. At the age of 27 he was five years younger than her, intelligent and arrogant. There had been something intangible between them since the interview, a certain something that contradicted the attraction.

It would have been wise to ignore this feeling, maybe even joke about it and make it look like a misguided kiss at an office party. But Sara wanted to take a break from her wisdom, and Mark too.

She glanced at Mark from her desk. He leafed through papers at his own desk. She picked up her phone and started typing.

Sara: Mark. There is an emergency in the office.

Sara watched. Mark read the message and his forehead curled in confusion. His eyes shot over the office and hit hers. He saw a smile on her face.

Mark: Hello Sara. What is the nature of your emergency?

Sara: Very soon there will be an unannounced fire practice.

Mark: ... really?

Sara: Yes. Everyone will leave. Fast.

Mark: So the office will be empty ...

Sara: Two of us should stay behind to make sure everyone goes outside safely. I've just promoted you to Deputy Fire Officer. Are you up to the task?

Mark: There's only one way to find that out.

Sara stood up slowly with a sneaky smile on her face, casually walked to the wall, grabbed the lever for the fire alarm and pulled it down. Suddenly the office was filled with noise as the alarm sounded and everyone started running out of their offices.

Sara stood at the fire-escape door, holding it open and pushing her colleagues out one by one like paratroopers from an airplane. Mark was the last and before he could go, she slammed the door. It was just her and him in the noisy, empty office.

She pushed him against the door and took him by the tie, pulled him to her and without saying a word, she started to kiss him. They kissed passionately. He put his hand on her head, pulled on her hair and pressed his weight on her.

Suddenly cold water came on them like rain. The cool water spilled over her, drowning the scent of his aftershave and leaving his white shirt hanging from his tall, slender body. With one hand she explored his body and with the other she unbuttoned her pants and pushed her hand inside.

Mark stepped back, still holding her hair and watching her pleasure. He listened to her breathing and the growing pleasure of her body.

"We only have five minutes," she almost whispered to herself, "before the fire department arrives." Sara said. "You have to fuck me and you have to do it now."

She pulled down her suit pants. She stood in high heels and dark stockings. With her free hand, she quickly undid Mark's belt and zipper and found his hard and thick cock. She pulled it out and stroked it.

As she stroked, he pulled her towards him and lifted her leg at the level of his hip. He held Sara's leg around him and felt her wet vagina glint as she carefully inserted his stiff member into him.

She gasped as he took control and gradually pushed slowly inward. She wanted to have everything from him immediately and she was not ready to wait. She began to rub and press him up and down. Mark lifted her leg a little higher so that she was on tiptoe. Sara could feel his strength, he basically picked her up off the floor and pushed her against the door as if he was piercing her with it.

Her legs fainted as a familiar wave of pleasure hit her body and she began to hit his bumps with her own as she came closer and closer. The waves of pleasure began to rise and develop into physical cramps.

Sara's fingernails scratched Mark's neck. With the other hand, she pleasured herself, and her legs became weaker with each finger movement.

Their eyes were closed, their mouths open, they were soaking wet and moaned loudly.

At last Sara let the wave crash down on her and every muscle got stiff. Hot convulsions shattered her whole body. The cramps seized and massaged Mark's cock inside her, causing him to lose control as he reached his climax in her orgasm-plagued body.

Exhausted, they smiled at each other. The sounds of the alarms returned as they came to.

They pressed their lips together, kissed and dressed quickly. Getting her hair and clothes on in time as the fire department arrived.

When the fire department arrived, it was time to go. After all, Sara always had a deadline.

Did you like the book? I'm looking forward to a review because that really helps me a lot. So, I can either improve something or appreciate that you have read my book and would like to thank me for your time.

Thank you, very much and good luck.

Disclaimer:

The author reserves the right not to be responsible for the topicality, correctness, completeness or quality of the information provided and other information.

Liability claims against the author, which refer to material or immaterial nature, which were caused by the use or non-use of the information provided or by the use of incorrect and incomplete information, are excluded, unless the part of the car demonstrably intentional or gross negligent fault exists. All information has been researched by the author with the utmost care and to the best of his knowledge and belief or reflects his own opinion. The content of the book may not suit every reader, and its implementation is at your own risk. There is no guarantee that everything will work exactly the same for every reader. The author and / or publisher cannot accept liability for any damages of any kind for any legal reason.

© / Copyright: 2018

Cortney Manocchia

1st edition

Self-published

Print: Amazon Media EU S.à.r.l., 5 Rue Plaetis, L-2338, Luxembourg

Contact: Cortney Mannochia

c/o AutorenServices.de

König-Konrad-Str. 22

36039 Fulda

Cover Photo: depositphotos.com

The work including its parts is protected by copyright. Any use is prohibited without the consent of the publisher and the author. This applies in particular to electronic or other duplication, translation, distribution and public disclosure. Bibliographic information of the German National Library: The German National Library lists this publication in the German National bibliography; Detailed bibliographic data are available on the Internet at http://dnb.d-nb.de

Manufactured by Amazon.ca
Acheson, AB